FOLLOW ME TO THE YEW TREE

DESIRÉE M. NICCOLI

For the grandmother I never got to meet.
And for my mom.

AUTHOR'S NOTE

This book is deeply personal. It's my first time writing a character with Ulcerative Colitis, something I have myself, and my grandmother had before me.

I never got to meet her.

She had a severe case that developed into colon cancer, but by the time they caught it, it was too late. She was forty-two when she died, leaving behind a husband, three children, a sister, and both her parents.

It's a loss my mother still feels keenly to this day.

My grandmother taught me how much you can miss a person you've never met. There's a deep longing in my heart to know her, in whatever way I can. When I released my first book, I learned that she read romance novels, and knowing that we have something so beloved in common makes me feel closer to her. I hope this one makes her proud.

Follow Me to the Yew Tree is intended to pack an emotional punch. It'll be heartbreaking at times, but I promise there's a happily-ever-after, because believe me when I say, I know how important that is.

CONTENT INFORMATION

You should always feel confident and safe when reading a book. As such, I've included a list of content information. If you have any concerns about the contents of this book, please be sure to check this list first.

This book contains sexual content. It is not intended for anyone under the legal age of adulthood. All characters depicted in sexual situations herein are over 18 years of age.

Other sensitive content within this book, includes, but is not limited to, near death experiences, grief, brief suicide ideation, mentions of war, Death, murder, and chronic illness (ulcerative colitis, cancer is briefly mentioned but ultimately not terminal).

CHAPTER 1

SPRING 1816, ENGLISH COUNTRYSIDE

I'm a long way from home.

I've exchanged Éire's rugged coast for a far-swept moor, and I don't know why I've been sent, only that I'm needed. And I'm nothing if not a faithful servant.

The road's been quiet—I haven't seen another soul in days—but now there's a lone man on horseback heading West, toward me.

All he has is what can be carried on his horse—bedroll, canvas tent, a saddle bag presumably filled with provisions. A cutlass dangles from one hip, a pistol is strapped to the other, and I've met enough sailors to know they are Navy-issue.

Auburn curls frosted white roll across his brow, ruffled by the breeze, the first splotch of color upon a drab landscape. With proper sunlight, the moor's green and purple grasses might've been better served, but today it's overcast and drizzling.

He tips his head in polite greeting, the small gold hoop in his ear catching the muted light. To say it glinted would be generous. Compared to the tattered, blue frock coat he wears with scuffed navy buttons and cuffs frayed and salt stained, or the tarnished compass that hangs from his belt, it's the most polished thing about him.

He doesn't smile as our eyes meet, and yet a gentle wave of

warmth settles in my chest, dripping slow and syrupy as honey. It's a bizarre sensation. Usually, when I find the one I'm meant to meet, the emotions strike cold and harsh. Why this is different, I can't say, and it doesn't begin to make any more sense even as a glowing vision follows.

It hits so suddenly my eyes swim with tears, as if I've dared to stare at the sun. Squinting and blinking doesn't help, but eventually my sight clears on its own, giving way to two distinctly recognizable figures.

They stand beneath the twisted boughs of a tree, their hands clasped, and heads bowed, backlit by an early morning sun. Beneath their feet, the moor grasses are still damp and glittering with dew.

Years of knowing imbue that touch, one of people whose understanding is marrow deep. And maybe that explains why their clothing is unfamiliar. Why it displays a scandalous amount of skin neither acknowledge. It's a glimpse at the times to come, a time when fabric molds and accentuates the body rather than hides it.

His lips curl into a sweet smile as he gazes at her mouth. Whatever he whispers brings a bright flush to her pale white cheeks, but she rises on her toes, boldly closing the distance. Her raven-dark hair is ever shifting, blown about on some ghostly breeze, and her eyes are a paler green than the Lily of the Valley that grows in the tree's shade.

He captures her face in both hands, the words "Hold Fast" inked across his fingers, sailors tattoos, as much a part of him as the calluses on his palm that now scrape across her cheeks. It's not the first time they've done this, but he slowly sips at her mouth, savoring her like it is, stroking the column of her throat with his thumbs. It's a tender dance of lips pursued by the languid glide of tongue, and the easy tempo endures even when he presses her against the tree, trapping her body with his own. The way he sucks her lower lip into his mouth, tugging lightly with his teeth, is so deliciously obscene, it's a surprise when he abruptly pulls away, leaving her red and swollen.

His eyes hold hers as he sucks two of his fingers into his mouth, cheeks hollowing out, before pulling the wet digits free and reaching down. It takes so very little effort to get beneath the skirt she wears. A garment that falls above the knee, not below.

Everything is quiet save for birdsong and soft, hitched gasps.

The vision's gone in a flash, a snapshot in time that leaves me breathless and stunned. It takes me a moment too long to realize I've been given a glimpse of the future. Of *my* future.

I see much but never something intimate. And never for me.

My horse whickers nervously, yanking me back into the present. I pat its neck, murmuring soothing words, even as my cheeks burn. "There, there. All is well."

I've never had reason to doubt my visions before, but if this one's to be trusted, the frowning man on the road ahead is my paramour-to-be.

Is this why I was sent? A reward for my centuries of faithful service? A balm to ease the weight of endless days and the long road ahead?

Hope burns bright in my chest. After witnessing so much pain and suffering, here's finally something good to hold onto. Someone to cherish, to keep. To call my own.

Love is the greatest gift of all, and if it's been gifted to me, I am well-appreciated indeed. All these long centuries spent grieving may finally be worth something, culminating to this moment.

Our horses draw near. I'm close enough to the man that I spy the constellation of freckles spanning his nose and the slight widening of dark brown eyes. Perhaps I stare too long because he hastily looks away, eyes bashfully averted, weather- and age-worn cheeks blooming a rosy color.

He couldn't have seen the vision. Could he?

Glancing down at myself, I'm quickly reminded of the fact that my long skirts are pulled up in front, revealing the men's riding trousers worn underneath. No skin is exposed, but well-regarded ladies don't dress as such.

There's nothing for it. Comfort and practicality must supersede some conventions.

I clear my throat and say, "Tráthnóna maith."

He looks up, surprised. Perhaps it's been a long time since he's heard the language of home. Seems just like the sort of thing a British naval officer would forbid, and I mourn the loss. "Tráthnóna maith." The surprise quickly dissipates, replaced by a flash of grim, troubled panic before falling into a more neutral expression. Did he not want to be recognized? "You're a long way from home."

"So are you."

A pause. His horse snorts, impatiently side-stepping.

"How did you know?" he asks.

"I had a feeling." What I don't say is that I wouldn't be here in this foreign country, sent to find him, if we didn't share a homeland. Éire, the place the English call *Ireland*.

A dark pallor drops over his face, obscuring his features in shadow. It's not an expression, or a change in mood, but a sign. A sign only I can see, and the warm feeling in my chest chills. He's not the first I've seen bearing such a portend, not by far, and he won't be the last. But after that beautiful, promising vision, I thought he was meant to be mine.

I thought I had a future that wasn't only steeped in sorrow.

I never should've assumed this meeting would end any differently than what's come before, that the one I serve would deign to bestow a gift. One pretty vision doesn't mean I know the man, or have any right to him, but to dangle hope and possibility in front of me like this, only to yank it away is unusually cruel.

It's all I can do to keep my voice even when I ask, "What's your name, sailor?"

His jaw clenches, and a haunted look steals the light from his eyes. "Don't."

I stiffen, taking him in. His eyes all at once turn wary and weary. He's a bit paler, too, beneath the damning shadow that hovers over his face.

"I'm not...I didn't choose that," he says.

I know that look. I've seen it before.

Many young men were impressed into His Majesty's Royal Navy during the Napoleonic Wars. Some are returning, but many will not. Just knowing this is the pain his past holds, calls to the part of me that wants to offer comfort, but never can. That doesn't mean I won't try. "I'm sorry. How long?"

"Too long. Enough to appoint me Gunner on a Man O' War."

"I take it that's not an easy accomplishment."

"From landsmen? Shouldn't've been possible, but enough men die on a ship, and someone's got to step in, take a place they never would've filled before. Many years of learning the hard way and eventually someone notices and decides it's worth something."

"Was it worth something to you?" I ask softly. In this, his opinion is the only one that matters.

He gives the question some thought, brows pinched, before answering, "Better pension, maybe." He frowns. "But I don't consider the proficiency of my position an accomplishment."

More death.

We're quiet for a long while, wind whipping about the moor grasses. I watch them sway. They remind me of waves, and I wonder if that thought crosses his mind, too.

"Elin," he says after a time. "That's my name. Da was an Englishman with a sense of humor." He runs a hand through his curls, burnished red against roughened, inked knuckles. "Like the sound, though."

A grown man with a name usually given to girls. While it's Welsh for "shining light," I can't decide if his father's humor is cruel or something else, but I like the sound, too, despite it.

Nodding to his horse, I say, "You're taking the long way home."

"If I never see another ship again, it will be too soon." There's a hint of wry humor to his words, a reluctant acknowledgement that he will eventually have to set sail again if he's to make it the rest of the way home, hopping from one island to the next.

"It must be a relief to be on solid ground again." It's not a particularly insightful response, but it's the first one to come to mind, and I find myself wanting to hear more of his voice and its gruff timbre.

Tipping his head back, and baring his face to the sky, Elin breathes in deep, serenity falling over his features. It's an open expression that softens the lines of his face, shaving away years of hardship, making him almost beautiful. When he finds my eyes once more, his are glittering coals closer to onyx than brown. "It's all I've wanted, even if it's not my own."

We're quiet a moment before Elin asks, "How is it at home, now that the war's done?" His voice is hesitant, as if he's afraid to know the answer.

I wish I could assuage his fears, but he's right to be worried.

Our country is in recession.

Manufacturing has decreased. Merchants are falling bankrupt, leaving so many unemployed, and what employment there still is comes at the cost of steeply slashed wages.

During the war, Éire supplied the English with beef, pork, and grain, but now that Napoleon has been defeated, competition from foreign exporters has made our trade dismal. Éire is no longer England's sole granary, and with the demand down, our farmers are already suffering. And so, so many of our people are farmers.

His expression darkens. My lack of a ready answer is telling. "It's not good, is it?"

"No, it's not." And even harder times ahead. It's a pattern with which I'm woefully familiar; centuries of living have taught me that war, famine, plague, and death are frequently grim companions.

Crop failure is coming. The next two years will yield so little, the people will dig out and eat their seed potatoes in desperation and be forced to scrounge for nettles and wild vegetables, whatever they can do to put something in their aching bellies. But it won't be enough.

It's a future filled with so many ghostly faces, people with sunken cheeks, and hollow, haunted eyes. If starvation doesn't claim them, fever and disease will.

"It's difficult to find work," I add, reluctantly. As a frequent bearer of bad news, you'd think I'd be used to it, but I loathe sharing this information. His homecoming should be a cause for celebration, joy, not despair. "Manufacturing and farming's not looking good."

He sighs. "Not sure they'll be keen, but I suppose the lads coming home can be fishermen."

I wince, and he notices, jaw clenching. "That, too?" he asks.

"Afraid so."

His expression is grim, resigned. "Seems the war has found a way to keep killing us after all."

I wish I could offer him comforting words, some sort of reassurance, but I've none to give. There's nothing left to do but march forward and make the very best of it as we can. I gesture behind me from the way I came. "I was just about to turn around. Mind if I join you?"

Elin tenses, his horse pawing at the ground. "Suppose you must, if we're headed the same way."

So much for clasped hands and heated kisses. I've no right to feel hurt by his lack of enthusiasm, but it stings, nonetheless. With a light jerk on the reins in my hands, I spin my mount around to lead the way. "I'm not such bad company." Might not be what he's expecting, a lone woman on an unmarked road, but I'm not unpleasant, and we share a language and a homeland.

He follows. "I meant no offense. It's just, I've traveled a long time alone."

If his crew didn't count—those that survived, that is—it must've been a long time indeed. My feelings aren't made of stone, but I take his meaning.

We ride in silence, miles passing through mountain and glen, the light of an already dim sky falling toward night. It's a peaceful kind of quiet, the kind that should only come from knowing someone a long time, or perhaps the things Elin has seen have made his spirit as old as mine.

As the sun dips near the horizon, my new travel companion brings his horse to a stop.

"Let's make camp." He angles toward a copse of trees, as if called by instinct to buttress against something firm, rather than boldly claiming open ground.

The shadowy pallor still hangs over his face, a grim warning of doom to come, but it hasn't worsened. Whatever's coming isn't imminent. Not yet anyway.

Casting a surveying look around just to be sure, I sense nothing amiss and follow without a word. Here is as good as any.

Elin takes the lead, tending to the horses and setting up a simple, canvas tent. He tackles each task swiftly and efficiently, the years at sea having done nothing to dull his landside skills.

He's busy unfurling a bedroll when he says, "I can take one side, you the other."

A generous offer to a stranger. Or maybe it's because I'm a woman and some chivalrous need dictates the gesture. As I unstrap the bedroll from my saddle, I feel the weight of his eyes on me, their presence warming me from behind. I'm not sure why I like that he looks, or why I like it even more that he doesn't avert his gaze when I turn around, his assessment continuing from a comfortable distance away.

"What brings you out here?" He watches me carefully, cautiously, like he might not wholly trust my intentions.

My inner turmoil returns. He's right to be wary. Why had I been sent? And what good were visions of a future that would never come true?

"I haven't figured that out yet." It's evasive, but also the truth as I know it, and I want to put him at ease, even if I'm beset by uncertainty. "But it's nice to have company for once."

A tiny smile lifts the corners of his lips, so it must work. "You wander often?"

"Spent a lot of time along Éire's east coast—Wicklow, Dublin— wherever I'm needed. I'm part of a courier service of sorts."

His brow ticks up a fraction. "Would I know it?" There's something teasing now about his tone.

I shrug.

"Do you like what you do?"

"Depends on the day. These are hard times. But on the good ones, I like to think I'm preparing people, letting them know what's to come. No one likes to be completely caught off guard."

Elin's smile fades. "No, I don't think we do."

While I arrange my bedroll inside the tent, contemplating overlong on the narrow space between mine and his, he gathers wood and builds a fire. By the time he's done a sheen of sweat coats his forehead, his cheeks pale. Before I can ask if he's feeling okay, he curtly excuses himself, snatching a saddle bag from the ground as he stalks tightly away into the dark of night.

Some call of nature beckons him away, but it isn't any of my business.

When he returns, he seems less strained, but his color hasn't returned, and his movements seem heavier. I dig into my rations. The bread I hand him in small chunks shouldn't be as fresh as it is, but he doesn't question it. Just murmurs his thanks and takes the first piece, popping it into his mouth, eyes closing, before chewing and swallowing. Bits of smoked, dried meat follow.

He eats a little but declines the rest. "I'm turning in."

There's no reason to sit here alone, not when curiosity about this man pulls at my chest.

He doesn't even turn around, just holds open the tent flap to let me in after him.

We shuck our shoes and lay down, tucking into our separate spaces—him on the left, me the right. Under the cover of my blanket, I slip out of the men's trousers, and though I try to be discreet about it, Elin's skyward stare is much too deliberate, his cheeks pink. Something about his shyness plucks at my heartstrings. There's so little between us in this shared space, and for all that society would consider me a woman of ill-repute just for the pragmatic way I dress, this land-starved sailor is respecting my privacy.

Even though it's not me who's shy, I leave the rest of my clothing be, and settle in.

Elin's lashes flutter, then fall closed, and he does a little shimmy getting into a more comfortable position.

We are close. So close I can feel his heat. I'd only need to turn over my arm to touch him, but I don't.

His breathing softens, deepens. Just when I think he's fallen asleep, he asks, "What's your name?"

"I've had many."

"Your favorite?"

I think a moment. "Éireann."

"Will I see you in the morning?"

An odd question. Where was there to go in the middle of the night? Did he think I was a thief? That I would steal his things and run off while he slept? Surely, he wouldn't have invited me to sleep next to him if he suspected that. "You'll see me in the morning."

Burrowing beneath his blanket, he turns over, back facing me. I know there's trust in that, but it makes my heart twinge, nonetheless. "In that case, oíche mhaith, Éireann."

"Oíche mhaith."

CHAPTER 2

A pressure on my bladder rouses me, but I pull up my blanket to cover my nose against the early morning chill. I'm reluctant to crack open my eyes, because the moment I do the pleasant dream I had will be gone.

"Be very still." Elin's voice is calm and quiet but firm.

My eyes fly open.

He's crouched beside me, a finger pressed to his lips. The shadowy pallor over his face is still there, but it hasn't worsened overnight, which eases some of my worry. "We've got company," he murmurs. "But I've got you. Just be very still."

And then I feel it. A wriggling between my left leg and the crease made by the tent's canvas and the ground. Without so much as twitching a muscle, my gaze dips down. There's an adder tucked half in, half out of my sleeping roll. Hardy and long-living, I may be, but not invincible, and I'm one venomous bite away from a bad day.

"What should I do?"

Picking up his blanket, and holding it between his hands, Elin answers, "Just slowly slide toward me. Don't jostle or squish it."

I do as he says, slowly inching my body across the ground until I'm pressed against his legs in the cramped space. For all that I'm one false move away from being bitten, a small thrill tingles in my belly at the contact. The vision of his lips on mine, thumbs stroking my neck, infiltrates my thoughts, insistent I don't forget. And how could I? It haunted my dreams in the dead of night, the sweetest, most persistent torture.

"Okay, slowly sit up," he instructs, his eyes never leaving the snake.

When I've done it, he continues, "Now get up and back out of the tent."

I like the command of his voice, and the assurance that it gives. It keeps me calm. As long as he's here, I'm safe, and I desperately want to offer him the same in return.

The snake is indifferent to my exit, just slides the rest of its body into the warm spot I vacated. Elin gingerly backs out. Together, we stare at the tent awhile, saying nothing, the air brisk.

"Wanted my body heat." I shiver, rubbing my arms.

"Mm." He nods, draping his blanket around my shoulders. "Were you bit? Anything hurt?"

I shake my head.

"We should check, just in case."

Putting ample distance between myself and the tent, I sit down on the ground, and he follows, crossing his legs. As I pull up my skirt, just enough to expose my calf and lower thigh, pale white flesh on display, my heart skips a beat. If the future's to be trusted, he will one day see all this and more.

If he's tempted by what he sees, he doesn't show it.

Brow furrowed in studious concentration, Elin rubs his hands together, then cups them over his mouth, blowing hot air. He repeats this process a few more times. When he places his hands on me, one behind my knee, the other my calf, they're warm and assured. Although he'd averted his eyes to my partial undressing the night before, he's not shy now as he examines and rotates my leg, pausing once to brush a finger over two beauty marks north of my knee.

Determining them innocuous, he moves on, palms skimming bare flesh.

The skin-to-skin contact is more comforting than I could've ever imagined, and there's a pleasant, buzzing sensation racing up my limbs and settling in my chest. It's no wonder humans seek touch so arduously; Elin hasn't yet let go, and I'm already craving more.

"No bite marks," he concludes, knees cracking as he rises to his feet.

I lower my dress and hold out my hand. Even though I don't need the help, I'm a newly made glutton. His grasp is firm as he pulls me to my feet.

Clutching the ends of the blanket to my chest, I nod toward the tent. "Now what?"

"Snake stays as long as it wants," is all he says, before setting off to gather kindling.

We leave when the snake does. It's a later start than either of us intended, but we manage six miles by midday. Elin is a quiet companion, but I like his presence.

When he takes a drink from his canteen, and wordlessly passes it to me, I notice the shadowy pall over him has darkened.

Alarm stabs in my chest, my eyes swimming with unbidden tears. In my haste to dry them, I'm clumsy with the canteen and spill our water. There's a wail, too, building in my diaphragm that I forcibly suppress. A bad, bad sign.

"You okay?"

"Gnat in my eye," I lie, trying to discreetly scan our surroundings for a threat.

He offers a handkerchief, and I take it, making a show of wiping an eye.

The vision that follows is fuzzy at the edges—a clear sign what I see isn't set in stone, at least not yet. It's a warning, and one I know I should convey, to give him time to prepare. It's why I'm here, after all, why I must've been assigned to him, but this can't be the end, not when we've barely begun. And not after all he's endured. To survive a war only to die on the journey home, that's not fate, it's cruelty. There should be so much life ahead of him to live. He deserves so much more than what this one is giving him.

But what if...

What if there's a silver lining to these visions? What if knowing what will happen ahead of time means I can stop it? What if I can save Elin?

It's not a thought I've had before. But I have to try.

There's two ways what comes next could play out, three if I'm quick enough.

But before the vision fully clears from my eyes, and before I can warn him, Elin is shouting. His horse rears, spooked by the snake I now know to be slithering through the heather around its hooves.

"Elin!" I yell as his horse bolts, unresponsive to his commands.

This only ends in tragedy if I don't stop it.

Dropping the canteen to grab my reins, I kick my horse into a hard sprint, leaning forward and low, giving it its head.

A dark, familiar voice whispers in my ear. *"Meddling with fate, are we?"*

"Not here, not now," I hiss through gritted teeth. Only I can hear this voice. It belongs to the one I serve—the one who sent me to this country in the first place, saying there was someone I needed to meet, but was infuriatingly sparse on the details.

"What will be, will be."

"Please," I beg. "Not this way."

"All living things are mine to take. Or have you forgotten?"

Bitter tears leak from my eyes. Loss and grief are my constant companions, the question almost cruel. One doesn't serve Death for centuries, witnessing countless ends, and not keenly understand life's finality. "But you can't have this one."

A menacing chuckle. *"Can't I? Is this a wager or a challenge?"*

Anger rises in my chest, boiling hotter than the wail that's been threatening release. None of this is a game to me—Elin, my heart, the possibility of our future.

"Neither," I growl.

It's a conviction. A vow.

"Nice try. May the best one win." Death's glee scrapes my already frayed nerves, but there's no time to protest the gauntlet he's thrown, or this will be over before it starts.

Ahead, the horse veers right...

And because of my vision I know there's a jump the horse fails to make, laming itself and crushing Elin beneath it. But that's not what kills him. It's the rock that cracks open his skull upon impact.

"Come on, come on," I urge my horse, air stinging my eyes. It lengthens its strides, drawing on extra reserves, to close the distance. We turn wide, flanking, then cutting off the other horse. It swerves left, but with its momentum disrupted, I use the opportunity to corral it, grabbing its reins the first chance I get, slowing us all to a stop.

Elin smacks off my hand, hard. It stings, but before I can snap at him for his ingratitude, he growls, "If my horse bolts again, he'll yank your goddamned arm out of its socket."

Startled, the biting comment hanging on the tip of my tongue dies there. I was so focused on saving his life, I became careless with my own wellbeing.

Elin's next words are ones of soothing for his snorting, stamping horse. He rubs large circles across its neck.

The creature eventually settles and lowers its head to eat grass.

The chase is over but my heart's still pounding, my mind's reeling, and I'm trying not to cry. I could have lost him, this man I only just met and am stupidly fated to love one day if he lives long enough. And while dodging this crisis gives me hope that maybe he will if I'm diligent enough—after all, Death's duties are infinite, and Elin is currently my sole priority—it's a wild and terrifying responsibility.

Getting my hand smacked and yelled at, even though I was doing something dangerous, keeps everything raw. It's too much all at once. Sucking in a shaky breath, I try not to let my face crumble as waves of emotion roll within me. "I just reacted."

"I know." His voice gentles. Something in the way he looks at me, really looks at me, gaze piercing and soft at the same time, makes me want to cry more, but I swallow my feelings.

He holds out his hand, and without thinking, I take it, the pressure grounding me. Whether or not he can see my self-control returning, he chooses now to say, "Thank you. I think you just saved me from a nasty fall."

"You're welcome," is all I manage, still raw.

"And I'm sorry." Head bowing, he cradles my hand in both of his, like he might a wounded bird, the touch so gentle. It's a stark contrast to the rest of his body which is tight with tension. "I shouldn't've smacked your hand or yelled. I may've lived a violent life, but that's not who I am, or who I want to be."

"You didn't do it in anger, and the situation called for urgency. There's a difference."

"Still." He lifts my hand to his lips, blowing lightly across the reddened skin, chasing away the lingering sting, before pressing a kiss to the spot. When his dark brown eyes meet mine, they're awash with regret. "Wasn't right."

I swallow thickly. It's not fear I feel when he touches me like this, but something tells me he won't accept forgiveness without penance. "Just don't do it again."

"Never," he promises, eyes searching mine. Waiting.

"You're going to have to make it up to me…" I venture.

He nods encouragingly, so I scramble to think of something to task him with. It's difficult, because from what I've seen, Elin already takes the lead in setting up and breaking down camp. If anything, it's me who needs to contribute more.

I rub my forehead. "Laundry duty?" It's already strenuous work with access to a stove for boiling water, a tub, a possing stick, and all the soap, starch, and stain-removing supplies one could need. But on the road? If we chance upon a stream, he'd be on his hands and knees scrubbing in cold water.

And yet, the tension in his shoulders finally relaxes, and a small smile breaks across his face, softening hardened, angular features. "I can do that."

"Good."

When he lets go of my hand, his tone is teasing. "Now, if you'll excuse me, and pardon my language, but that just about scared the shit out of me." He dismounts, taking a saddle bag with him, disappearing off into a cluster of trees. His exit is abrupt and borderline rude, but urgency must demand it.

It's a while before he comes back, but when he does, I've a much better handle on myself. "Sensitive stomach?"

"Bowel calamity," he replies with surprising honesty, placing a hand over his lower abdomen. "I've had it half my life. Sometimes it's no trouble, but when it flares up, and flares up something fierce…it's rather unpleasant."

"Unpleasant?"

"Can I be indelicate?" That's what he says, but what I hear is, "Can I trust you?"

I nod, sensibilities girded, and compassion armed.

"Somedays, I can't so much as sneeze or break wind without causing a catastrophe in my own goddamn trousers." It's harshly said, but more frustrated than embarrassed. "And there's nothing I can do about it. All the jarring and jostling from riding irritates it. And I've got to be careful about what I eat. Cheese? Too much brings regret. Coffee, too. But poorly cooked onions…" He grimaces. My face must betray my curiosity because he adds, "Bad bloat. Hurts a lot."

Ship life must've been a nightmare.

"That sounds miserable." I clasp his upper arm, hoping touch comforts more than words, because I'm not sure what else to say. He doesn't pull away. "What's in the saddle bag?"

"Bar o' soap. Extra water. Rags I won't miss."

No additional explanation is needed.

"I know we're strangers," I begin, thinking to thank him for his trust.

But he just shrugs, and says, "It's easier in the long run. There won't be any hiding it on the road."

It's true.

We stop five more times that day for Elin. After the third, he doesn't bother riding anymore, just walks beside his horse. Each time, he returns paler and paler, his expression a mixture of discomfort and frustrated defeat. And each time, my heart aches. I want to hug him, make him feel better, but we're just two strangers accepting each other's company on the road.

But I learned something invaluable today. If I could save him this once, I can save him again.

No, I *will* save him again. As many times as it takes.

I will thwart Death at every pass.

CHAPTER 3

Elin lays curled on his side, clutching his middle, and though he suffers in silence, his discomfort is a palpable thing in the tiny tent we share. It's been hours since we both turned in for the night. Hours of reluctant wakefulness.

I fumble in the dark to build a fire just so I can boil hot lemon water. It won't be much, but it's supposed to be good for digestion, and maybe having something hot in his stomach will help carry him away into sleep.

Getting the fire hot enough takes far longer than I'd like, but even if it only makes Elin feel a fraction better, it'll be worth the effort.

When it's ready, he takes the steaming cup I hand him and sips it without question. We're still as good as strangers, and yet, necessity and circumstance have built a tenuous bridge of trust between us. While Elin revealed his condition to me for practical reasons, that he allows me to care for him now feels significant. There's nothing I can do about the calamity that holds his body hostage, but if I can ease the hurts and discomforts at all, I will.

As soon as he finishes, I take his mug to boil him another cup.

I fill the small pot, and crouch down, adding twigs I've gathered to the fire.

"Where's your charge going, do you think?"

I startle so hard I jostle the pot, water sloshing over the edge.

"What are you talking about, he's right…" I look behind me, where Elin's laying inside the tent. Only now he's gone. I curse.

Death laughs.

Normally, I wouldn't've thought anything of it. Elin rushes off abruptly for privacy all the time. But Death has made note, which means I should, too.

A vision hits me hard and fast, drowning out all sense and sensation. I can't see, can't hear anything but the future before it unfolds.

And yet, I get up and run, tearing blindly through the moor grasses. The vision will clear soon, but there's no time to waste, not when I foresee Elin gasping, choking, clawing for air.

"Elin!" I yell. "Elin!"

"Don't trip."

My foot promptly catches on a rock, and I tumble forward, barely catching myself. The vision's already fading to reveal the world around me, an endless sea of grass in the black of night.

A cluster of Will o' Wisps, twinkling like fireflies in the night, flit lazily from our camp—Elin obediently following behind. If I don't catch him in time, they'll lead him into a bog with a deep peat mat that's hard to spot because of the plant life that grows on its surface.

He'll drown in stinking, sucking mud.

I pick up my skirts and run as fast as my legs will carry me, the ground growing soft and wet beneath my bare feet.

"Elin, stop!"

He doesn't falter, marching steadily onward.

The Wisps have got him well and truly entranced.

"Better hurry."

"Shut it."

He's knee deep when I reach him.

Grabbing him by the shoulders, I whirl him around. His body is so loose and languid there's no difficulty maneuvering him. "Elin, snap out of it." I shake, watching as light returns to his glassy, distant eyes.

He startles, water splashing at his feet, and then tenses, taking on a wide-legged stance. "We're taking on water!" His shout is uncomfortably loud in the quiet night, like it's meant to be heard above blustering wind and a raging sea. He reaches for something that isn't there. "Man the pumps!"

"Elin," I say again softly, cupping his cheek. "Look at me."

It takes two more tries, but he does, confusion writ across his face.

"We're not on a ship." I take one of his hands, tugging him toward solid ground. "We're on land, but you wandered into a bog."

He shakes his head, pressing the heel of his hand to his forehead. "There were these pretty, little lights hovering outside the tent. Tried catching one, but it darted just out of reach."

"Those were Will o' Wisps. Never follow them. They like making travelers lose their way." And lead them to their deaths, but I don't tell him the last bit.

Back at camp, we clean up our legs and feet before returning to bed. I watch the soft rise and fall of Elin's body as he falls asleep, and bring his blanket up around his shoulders, tucking him in.

Death is quiet, having no victory to gloat over.

But this is not a game, and nothing about this situation is amusing. To play with a life like this is cruel.

The Will o' Wisps return, cheeky little shits, but Elin's thankfully not awake to see them.

They'll not have him. Not tonight, not tomorrow, not ever.

Storming out of the tent, I lash out and grab one, squeezing it mercilessly in my hand, absorbing its energy. Its panic flickers once, twice, thrice before winking out of existence. The rest of the cluster scatters, racing off into the night lightning fast, and this time I'm certain they're gone for good.

They're not used to being prey.

Uneasy, I return to the tent and try to sleep. I'm plenty tired from our travels, but my latest vision haunts the back of my eyelids, torturously replaying Elin's drowning in a never-ending, macabre loop. Several times, I reach out to touch his back, making sure he's still there and breathing.

Knowing what happens before it does is as much a blessing as it is a curse, because to save Elin means I must watch him die first.

CHAPTER 4

Elin studies the sky. "Storm's coming."

The wind's picked up a bit, and the temperature's dropped. There's still a snatch of sun peeking through the clouds, but if anyone's going to have good storm-sense, it's this seasoned sailor.

Three days into our journey during England's rainy season, some bad weather was overdue.

Scoping the landscape for someplace to take shelter, I spot a sizeable structure ahead. At this distance, it's just a smudge on the landscape, but between its size, shape, the smoke billowing up from the chimney, and swaying sign out front, I'd wager it's an inn, the first we've seen.

"Look." I point, and Elin squints. "What about that?"

He thoughtfully rubs a hand over his chin. "Won't say no to a real bed."

"Here." I reach into my saddle bags and pass him a coin-filled purse. His brows raise at its heft, but he doesn't protest my implicit offer to put us up for the night and tucks it away into an inner coat pocket.

By the time we reach the inn, angry, dark clouds roll overhead, followed by a sinister rumble of thunder. The horses spook a bit, but after a quick exchange of coins, the groom on staff takes them into the inn's stables to be brushed down and fed.

Our belongings slung over our shoulders, we make for the inn, the loud clamor within spilling out from behind the closed door. Singing, swearing, crashing—we share a look, worried we're walking out of one storm and into another—but a flash of lightning overhead, chased by loud, bellowing thunder has us scurrying inside. We're barely in through the front door when rain begins to fall in thick sheets.

It's utter chaos on the inside.

A rough bunch of men, about ten armed to the teeth, have made themselves right at home in the dining area. Some sway and sing off key, belting out the words to a bawdy song, their tankards of ale sloshing over the brim. A few recklessly throw darts—a barmaid ducks with a startled shriek, narrowly avoiding one that's way off mark. Two men are brawling, bumping into tables, knocking over drinks. The one's got the other in a headlock, but they're both red-faced from laughter, so it appears playful.

For now.

The way the staff move silently about the room, serving food, wiping up messes, righting fallen chairs, all with their heads bowed and eyes carefully averted, making themselves as small and beneath notice as possible, makes it clear this isn't the usual crowd.

Behind the counter, the innkeeper hovers over a ledger, tugging at greying hair as he casts worried glances at the dining area, occasionally pausing to scratch a notation. He's so absorbed in both tasks that he doesn't notice our arrival.

Elin clears his throat. "Any rooms left?"

The innkeeper jumps, but his panicked expression is swiftly masked. Straightening his jacket, and smoothing a tremoring, liver-spotted hand down his well-starched shirt, he replies, "Several, actually."

Elin passes payment across the counter, his palm hiding the newly minted coins plucked from my purse, and I appreciate the wisdom in not drawing attention to how much money we carry. Discreetly, he tilts his head in the direction of the drunken ruffians. "Busy night."

The innkeeper leans across the counter, lowering his voice. "They're scaring off our other customers, but at least so far, they've been paying toward their tab. Just got to keep our heads down and weather out the night. But even if they weren't paying, I don't have the kind of manpower to run them off, and I'll not risk my staff."

Sharing a roof with belligerent, well-armed men promises trouble, and if we hadn't been chased in by the storm ourselves, I might've suggested we opt for sleeping in the rough again. But bad weather breeds necessity, and the shadowy pallor that's become a permanent fixture over Elin's face doesn't darken. That's enough to put my mind at ease about his immediate safety.

Elin continues conversing with the innkeeper. "How're your guest room locks?"

"They're good, brand new. But I'll be honest, if someone really means to get in, they can be picked."

Elin nods curtly, then turns to me, bending to whisper into my ear. A pleasant shiver races up my spine at the warm tickle of his breath. "I'll feel better if we share a room."

And truth be told, so would I, but more for his sake than mine. Every clomping set of footsteps on the stairs or rattling door latch would have me sitting up in bed, listening, and worry makes for poor sleep.

"We can share," I whisper back, meaning to reciprocate his discretion, but my gaze strays to his lips for the briefest, barest moment. I don't know why I looked, why I marked their pale color, their sensuous curve, or the singular brown freckle dotting the edge of his lower lip.

That his face hovers inches from mine is just an excuse.

His gaze darkens, something brewing in the abyss of his deep brown eyes, and it makes heat curl in my belly. When I swallow, his eyes dip down to watch the movement.

"Elin?"

He steps away suddenly, and I've no right to feel bereft, but I wish I hadn't shattered the moment. I wish he hadn't pulled away.

"I'll take one for my wife and I," he says to the innkeeper.

My wife. He just called me his *wife*.

Elin looks back at me over his shoulder, the slight uptick of his brow daring me to challenge him.

Should I be angry? Offended by the lie? Whatever his intentions in claiming me as his wife, how can I deny this harshly beautiful man whose future is woven with mine?

Cheeks burning, I barely register the innkeeper saying he'll send up food and hot water for bathing, complimentary to our stay, as an apology for having to share space with rowdy guests. My mind races at the implications of Elin's words. A ruse to protect my honor? The condition of a lady's reputation dictates her entire future, and while the circles I come from don't follow such conventions and won't care whether Elin and I are married, that's not something he would know, and it's rather sweet that he's considered my well-being.

Unless...

My stomach swoops at the possibility that safeguarding my reputation might not be the primary reason for the subterfuge. That Elin may intend to have me as a husband has a wife.

But that thought is quickly buried.

He's been so sick these past few days, and while his bowel calamity has given him some reprieve today, he's eaten very little and is still paler than I'd like.

No, this is just a story to avoid the innkeeper's judgment, cruel whispers from the staff, and shoddy service.

After pocketing our room key, Elin presses a kiss to my temple and takes my hand. That I tell myself it's only for show as he leads me up the stairs does little to quell the fluttering of my overeager heart.

The narrow hallway is quiet, our room toward the end.

I'm not fond of the close quarters, strategically speaking, but there's a secondary stairwell several doors down that might prove useful for a getaway should the situation downstairs get out of hand and migrate up here.

Elin drops my hand to unlock the door, letting us inside.

Rain pelts the panes of the room's singular window, the skies outside so dark it could be night. I hover in the threshold as Elin tosses his saddle bags onto the floor and begins lighting candles. It's just enough light to see that the room is small but clean with a bed for two and a modest desk and chair set.

I lock the door behind me and prop the desk chair under the latch, using it as a secondary measure for barring unwanted entry.

Elin nods his approval and begins unfurling his bedroll.

So much for continuing to play the part of a married couple.

While the confirmation of the ruse stings a little, I place my hands on my hips and pin him with a hard look. "There's more room in this bed than the tent we shared, so don't even think about sleeping on the floor, *husband*."

Elin blushes. "If I had another tent..."

"The one suits just fine."

"We've a roof over our heads, and a floor's easier than the ground."

"You stubborn man, who are you putting on an act for?" I throw up my hands. "Just share the damn bed with me."

A smile flirting on the edge of a smirk, ticks up the corner of his lips. "All right," he says with a small bow. "As the lady insists."

I whisk a pillow off the bed and throw it at him.

CHAPTER 5

Hot water and food are brought to our room, and Elin stands at the window, sipping on soup, his body in profile while I bathe. A flash of lightning illuminates his pale form, and for a single moment caught between light and shadow, he looks like a wraith. I shiver, despite the bath water's heat. Even if it's the last thing I do, that's a fate I'll do anything to make sure he avoids. And not just because he's my fated love, but because it's something I realize I should've been doing all along throughout the long centuries of my life.

Successfully saving Elin twice has taught me that.

A thunderous boom rattles the windowpane, but Elin calmly continues staring out into the empty blackness. I marvel at his composure until I remember he must've weathered far worse storms at sea. This inn with its sturdy roof and stone foundation must feel so safe compared to a rolling, pitching ship. No sails to man nor lines to haul while the sea does its damned best to swallow everything whole.

When he's had his fill, Elin sets the bowl down and crosses his arms, the ink on his knuckles visible in the dim light.

Gliding the bar of soap up my arm, I ask, "Why 'Hold Fast'?"

Still facing out, he leans against the window frame, crossing his legs at the ankles. "So much of my life has been wasted in service to a king and country that's not mine. And I watched so many crew mates get torn apart by cannonball fire. If not by the ball itself, then by the splinters blasted off the ship. What's worse is knowing I did that, too, to the men on the other end of our guns." He rests his temple to the window, breath fogging the glass, and his next words are so quiet I strain to hear them. "So often I wanted it to end. Sometimes I'd climb to the main topsail yard and think about flying." He turns over his hand, brushing a thumb along his inked knuckles. "This became my daily reminder to never let go."

The heavy confession stills my hands. I want to go to him, to hold him, but without a stitch of clothing, I don't dare. All I can do is tell him I'm grateful he's here.

"For what it's worth, I'm glad you held on."

"Me too," he answers, but his smile is wistful. "For as long as it lasts."

I frown. Surely his state of mind is better now that he's no longer sailing. "You're free to live your life as you choose…"

I can only see him in profile, but the look that falls over his face is so riddled with pain I immediately wish I could retract the words. I flounder for an appropriate apology, but I don't know how I offended him.

"I wish that were true." He turns his back to me, and I can no longer see any of his face.

I finish bathing and get ready for bed in cold, hard silence.

CHAPTER 6

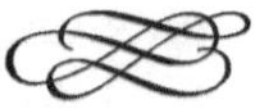

Arattling at the door jolts us both awake.

It's pitch black, but the mattress creaks as Elin rolls over, grabbing the pistol he stashed under his pillow before we climbed into bed, him taking the left side, me the right.

Just like on the road. So little time together, and we've already fallen into a routine.

"S'locked," someone slurs. "Key ain't working."

"Can have me out here, if you like, but it'll cost extra."

Clinking coins, rustling clothes, then a steady, rhythmic thumping at the door follows.

I suck in a surprised breath. "Elin, I think they're…"

"They are," he affirms gravely.

Thump, thump, thump, thump.

It's so utterly ridiculous, a giggle escapes me, and after two beats, Elin's rumbling laughter joins mine.

An enthusiastic series of grunts and moans and creaking wood follows.

Rolling over, I strike a match and light the bedside candle. We won't be getting any decent sleep while that's happening.

Elin's face is heavily shadowed in the meager light, but I don't miss his bemused expression. Returning his pistol to its place beneath the pillow, he flops back, arms crossed above his head. With a slight shake, he chuckles. "This could go on awhile."

The movement tosses his burnished curls, made fiery in the candlelight, and it's all I can do to keep myself from sweeping them from his eyes. Some are still damp from bathing, but most have dried, the springy type that bounces when you tug one and let go. If there wasn't a tupping couple just beyond our door, I might've done it, but I'm too afraid to touch him to a moaning chorus.

When I don't immediately respond, he extends the pinkie and thumb of his right hand and tilts it back toward his mouth, miming drinking from a bottle.

"Pardon?" Whatever point he's trying to make doesn't land.

He averts his eyes and clears his throat, awkwardness pinching his features. Is he embarrassed?

"What?" I prod.

He gives me a pained look.

Taking my pillow, I playfully smack him on the chest several times. "Tell me."

Huffing out a frustrated breath, he swipes it away and grumbles, "Fine. But don't go complaining when it ruffles your polite sensibilities."

The woman outside chooses that precise moment to let out a throaty moan.

I smirk, gesturing toward the door. "Consider my polite sensibilities already ruffled. And when have you ever heard me complain?"

He swipes both hands up his face, then pins me with a hard stare. "You sure you want to know?"

I lift my pillow again, and he snatches it from my hands. "Knock it off woman, I'm going to tell you."

"Get on with it already."

"When a man's had too much to drink, his..." The thumping at our door grows particularly savage. "His..."

Crossing my arms, I arc my brow. "His what?"

His expression is tortured. "Don't make me say it."

I throw up my hands. "Elin, if you don't say co—"

In a flash, he sits up in bed, cupping a hand over my mouth. The other cradles the nape of my neck. "Dammit Éireann, his bloody cock gets hard." He spits out the words angrily. "And it stays that way. Doesn't matter how beautiful the woman is in his arms, he won't finish."

My eyes are wide. I haven't done anything to exert myself, but I'm breathing hard, and so is he.

"Do you know what finishing means?"

I do, but I don't answer. The words are frozen on my tongue.

He leans in close, his hand all that keeps our lips apart. "It means," he continues, voice pitching low, "he can't spill his seed in her. Just goes on and on and on until he's too chafed and sore to keep it up."

Slowly, he slides his hand from my mouth, blazing a hot trail down my neck before coming to rest just above the swell of my breast. There's a challenge in his eyes when he asks, "Satisfied?" But the word is a warm caress, and I am a quivering bundle of longing and desire. All sound falls away. The couple at our door, the drunken revelry downstairs, the raging storm outside. All sound disappears save for the sound of Elin's ragged breath, his racing heart.

"Almost," I whisper.

He searches my eyes. What he's looking for, I don't know, but I don't want him to stop. "You've the palest green eyes I've ever seen," he murmurs softly, almost to himself. His thumb brushes over my cheek. "Barely the thought of green."

My lips ghost his, just the barest of touches, and his fingers curl into my raven-dark hair, a delicious tug that stokes the flames building within me. I arc into his heat, sink into the plush feel of his mouth. Just a taste and I'm lost. Or has he found the essence of me in a single, delicate kiss? I grasp the open neck of his linen shirt, the skin beneath smooth and warm and a beautiful tapestry of freckles, as numerous as there are stars in the sky, and I feel as grounded by him as carried away.

In his arms, I am the intrepid explorer, and he the compass, guiding me toward sweet oblivion.

I press into him, deepening the kiss, but with a sharp curse, he pulls away, withdrawing entirely, and my heart plummets straight to my stomach, leaving nothing but the chill room and bitter regret. Now I've ruined everything, and we're days yet from the end of our journey. Days that will be awkward and tense because I just *had* to kiss him.

He scrubs his hands over his face, the inked words "Hold Fast" mocking me in the dim light.

Elin let me go the moment he knew he could have me.

"I can't." And he sounds so agonized, it wrecks me. I consider making a run for it, even if it means pushing past our limb-locked neighbors, but he grabs my hands. So much emotion swims in the deep, dark pools of his eyes. "But God, I want to. Everything's willing —my mind, my heart, my soul—everything except my goddamned body. This condition I have—it makes me feel so sick and out of control and a downright bloody mess. Any kind of jostling..." He takes a deep breath. "You saw what it was like when we were out on the road."

It's in this moment I understand how my earlier comment hurt him. He'd survived the Napoleonic Wars and his Royal Navy service and was now well on his way home with an honorable discharge and a pension, but he wasn't free to live his life as he chose. Not really. Not when his own body betrayed him every single day.

Every day was a fight for survival, down to the words inked on his fingers.

"Can I hold you?" I ask softly.

His surprise is palpable, and that pierces me, too, that he'd expect rejection in return for his honesty. But the surprise quickly gives way to something warm and tender I can't identify. "I'd like that."

He lays down, and I curl around his back, cupping his body with mine. When I lay my palm upon his middle, I can feel through the fabric of his shirt how distended his belly is. My heart twinges again, and shift my palm upwards, but he catches my hand. "If it's okay with you, I wouldn't mind a little pressure there. No squeezing, but a little bit feels nice. Like you're holding me together."

My eyes mist at the thought—that I might actually be holding him together—and I snake my arm around him, using my forearm to give him that support. "I don't mind."

With a quick tug, he yanks his pillow down, laying half on top of it, and using it, I assume, for more support. His head falls on the mattress.

"Do you want to share mine?"

He nods, and raises his head, so I can slide my pillow evenly between us both.

There's something that needs to be said while we share these close quarters and the reality that there's no privacy here. And I need Elin to know that it's okay, no matter what.

Nose pressed to the groove of his back, where flesh meets spine, I say, "I don't frighten off easily, and I'm not squeamish."

It's my burden, and my duty to see the end before it comes. However, it comes.

I've seen people drawn and quartered, their bodies cracked and broken, their viscera strewn across muck limned streets. I've seen them disemboweled, desperately trying to hold in their guts as life drains away. I've seen hangings, and the way piss and shit expel from the body at death. And I've seen the softest bits of a person get pecked from the body by crows as they scream.

Countless women I've wailed for, only to watch them die at the hands of their husbands, a covetous, lecherous neighbor, or a pillaging marauder. And I've seen them bleed out in childbirth almost as many times as I've seen them abandoned after a botched abortion, alone and discarded and afraid.

And I've wailed for those condemned for just being their true selves. Because being different, being special, is always a sin to those who'd rather hold hate in their hearts than try to understand.

There are so many ways to die, I'll never shame a person for what their bodies must do, what struggles they must endure, to live.

"I'm also a deep sleeper," I continue. "So, if you wake up in the middle of the night and think the latrines out back are going to be too far away, there's a chamber pot beneath the bed and absolutely nothing to be ashamed about using it."

There. It was said.

Elin tenses, then snorts. "Saying I can freely shit my guts out in front of you?"

He jests, but I see the humor for what it is—armor.

"I'm being serious, Elin. I'm not going to judge or think less of you or some other such nonsense."

He falls quiet. I don't think he's going to respond until he hugs my arm to him and whispers, "Thank you."

Tomorrow, assuming the storm passes, we'll be on the road again. And while I don't know yet what our travels will bring, this man will live, dammit.

I don't care what it takes.

CHAPTER 7

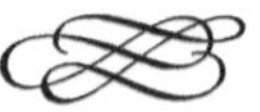

It's too early for drinking, but one of the men from last night's ruffian group is already tossed. That, or he never stopped, which seems most likely.

"Eh, miss," he slurs. Disheveled brown hair falls to his shoulders, a red, cockeyed neckerchief tied loosely about his neck. His eyes are glassy and bloodshot, and his breath, unsurprisingly, reeks of booze. "Got any coin to spare?"

A spoon of porridge is halfway to my mouth when he says this. Elin and I came down to the inn's dining room at daybreak, but while I savored my breakfast, he scarfed down his, eager to get back on the road. He's currently in the stables saddling up our horses.

"No." I go back to eating. Maybe if I ignore him, he'll go away.

"Now, I know that can't be true." He gestures to me with his tankard, ale sloshing over the side. I scoot away a fraction, narrowly avoiding being splashed. "You're dressed too well."

So much for dissuading him.

He stumbles forward, reaching for my dress pockets. I know this for what it is—a drunken man's poor, foolish attempt to rob me, but to anyone else, it would appear he's groping for other nefarious reasons.

I glance around to see if anyone's watching. There's the innkeeper and a barmaid, but their backs are turned as they wipe out glasses with rags and discuss the boon of falling food prices in Ireland. *The English getting cheap, imported food means our farmers suffer.*

But I tuck that anger away for later and seize on the fact that there's no witnesses to see what I do next.

I grab the man's hand in a bruising grip, making him yelp. I'm about to break his bones and knock him unconscious when Elin comes bursting in through the door.

His eyes narrow, rage and lethal intent claiming his usually unflappable composure. I've never seen him so ferocious. Might this be what he looked like on the deck of a ship, charging the enemy crew, a cutlass in hand? Or in the moments before lighting the first fuse that sets in motion a volley of cannonball fire?

Elin's flushed so red I fear he may combust on the spot. And then he springs. In seconds, he's rushed the man, tearing him off me and shoving him away.

The man reels back, colliding with a neighboring table, spilling most of his drink.

"Keep your hands off her," Elin growls.

The ruffian slams his tankard down on the table, fury menacing his features. He lurches forward, chest puffed out. "And what are you going to do about it?" His arm's drawn back, fingers dancing along his hip.

I toss a coin purse onto the table, and shoot out of my chair, knocking it over. "Let's just go."

I push Elin back, and he turns his glare on me. "What are you…"

"Come on," I grind out, grabbing him by the wrist and dragging him outside. The sooner we get away from here the better.

Behind us, the ruffian laughs, and with a clink of coin, yells, "Bar wench, more beer!"

I slam the door shut behind us.

Elin whirls on me, gesturing sharply toward the inn. "Why'd you do that?" he seethes.

"He was going to pull a knife on you." I mime the stance, fingers dancing near a concealed weapon.

"You don't think I knew that?"

"And what, you were just going to fight him anyway?"

"He was pawing at your skirts."

"He only wanted my coin purse."

"Oh, is that all?" Elin's laugh is bitter. "Well, that changes things. Maybe I should go back in and apologize for overreacting."

"Stop it. That's not funny. You could've gotten hurt, and no amount of money is worth that."

"I can handle my way around a fight. I've spent the last twelve years on a warship. You don't think I can take on a drunk with a knife?"

"I had a bad gut feeling."

"*You* had a bad gut feeling?"

I wince, regretting the choice of words. "Elin, I'm sorry. I didn't mean…"

"I'm sick, not helpless. And because you seem to have forgotten, I was perfectly fine keeping myself alive before you showed up." He storms off, swearing as he fetches his horse. And notably not mine.

"Elin?"

Ignoring me, he swings up onto his mount, fury hardening his features.

"Elin?" I repeat, a little more desperately.

He kicks his horse's sides and doesn't look at me once as he gallops off.

CHAPTER 8

I follow at a distance, giving Elin space to cool, but I'm sick to my stomach with regret. The poor choice of words, the over-stepping.

Knowing the ruffian was going to pull a knife wasn't premonition. That was just reading body language. If they'd fought, Elin might've gotten hurt, but it wouldn't have killed him. I could've, and maybe should've let it play out, but dammit, I didn't want him to get hurt either. And at this point, intervening has become instinct.

And now he wants nothing to do with me.

Bollocks, I know he isn't helpless. The furthest from, but we are at odds with Death himself, and no mortal can withstand that summons when it comes due.

At nightfall, I watch him set camp from afar, no longer welcome. I've no tent of my own, so I unsaddle my horse, and when she lays down, I follow, resting my back against her side.

To think, only last night I'd thought a simple kiss had ruined things, and then I had to go and make it all worse, digging a deeper and wider hole between us. How could I have allowed myself to mess up this badly? I've been so desperate to save Elin, to keep him alive. If my own thoughtless actions drive him into Death's arms, because I'm not near enough to warn him, it'll haunt me forever.

I hug my knees to my chest, my head bowed between the fold of my arms, feeling utterly wretched as I begin to cry. What a colossal mess I've made of things.

The ground crunches as footsteps approach, but I don't look up, hiding my shame.

A hand rests on my quaking shoulder, and I don't need to see to know it's Elin. We're alone, after all. Just two people out here beneath the starry night sky. "I'm sorry," he says, dropping to the ground beside me. "I shouldn't have yelled or left you like that."

My sniffling is pathetic, and I've no right to self-pity, but I can't seem to stop. "I'm sorry, too," I whisper. Any more volume and it'd be an ugly croak. Once I've started, I can't stop; this runaway train of emotions will only end in collision, and I'm not brave enough to let him see. "I hurt you," I choke out, the words thick and heavy in my throat. Cowardly though I am, I need to at least acknowledge something of my wrongdoing.

"My pride, maybe. Felt like a child who'd needed protection, but I was scared, too, for your safety. Still, I wish I hadn't lashed out like that. I knew it came from a place of caring."

All I can manage is a firm nod. I want to tell him again that I'm sorry, that I'll be more considerate of his capabilities, and not diminish him, but if there's danger, real danger, I can't stand aside and let fate have him. Ignoring my instincts is one thing. Ignoring my premonitions means certain death.

"Can I hold you?" he asks softly.

I'm the one at fault, and yet, he's the one consoling me. It makes me feel awful, but I accept it, and when his arms wrap around me, pulling me close, I soak in the comfort of his body. There's a part of me, too, that feels relief for not wrecking things beyond repair.

When my sobbing subsides, he presses a kiss to the top of my head and combs the hair away from my tear-streaked face. "Will you come back with me?"

I nod again, still not trusting my voice to remain steady.

He helps me to my feet, and once I'm stable, he patiently waits as I brush bits of twigs and leaves off my skirts. My eyes are still averted.

"Éireann," he says, but I can't look. Not when I've just stopped crying. If I meet his eyes, I'll begin anew.

"Éireann," he repeats, in a tone no doubt once used on the sailors under his command. "Look at me."

I do, and as predicted, the tears well again, messily spilling over.

He cups my cheeks, thumbing them dry, the look in his eyes devastatingly tender. "Don't hide from me, whether I'm the reason for these or not."

"But why?" No doubt my eyes are red and puffy, and I sniff to keep my nose from running. If how I feel is any indication, I must look utterly wretched.

"So, I can do this." He leans in, kissing one cheek, then the other. But he isn't done. He continues to my forehead and each of my temples, even the tip of my nose. Every press of his lips is precious—one more touch I never thought I'd have—and every one soothes away the hurts, warmth blooming where there'd been regret before.

His kisses fall to my jaw, then brush the round of my chin, before landing on my lips, firm and sure but quick. It's a chaste kiss. There's no heat, no exploration, and yet it startles away the lingering tears and kindles a fire in my belly.

I hold his gaze, greedily drinking it in, and he smiles. "There you are," he says.

"You shouldn't do that." I say, touching my lips.

"Do what?"

"Kiss me like that."

"And how did I kiss you?" The corner of his mouth quirks, but his eyes are serious, almost solemn.

I squeeze my eyes shut for a moment, the bittersweet burn of yearning filling my chest. "Like I could have you."

His eyes darken, and he steps closer. "Who says you can't?" There's a hunger in his expression, one I've never seen before, and it contrasts with the gentle way he tucks a flyaway behind my ear, caressing the outer ridge as he goes.

"You did," I fire back, a little more hotly than intended. This time it's frustrated tears that mist my eyes, but I don't look away. I promised not to hide, and he should know my heart is as good as his, but it's not for toying with.

"That's not what I said." He bends close, resting his forehead to mine, as his fingers entwine around strands of my raven-dark hair. "I said I couldn't fuck you, not that I wouldn't." His voice is heavy with want as his hands clench, then unclench, delivering just a slight tug at my roots. It's like he wants to possess me, to claim me, and it's taking everything to hold back, but his self-control is a tenuous, snappable thing. "God, I desperately want to. Should I prove it to you?"

Before I can respond, he takes my hand, bringing it down. The grip's loose, so I can pull away at any time, but I don't want to. The promise is too tantalizing.

Our breath hitches collectively when my palm meets the hard bulge at the front of his trousers. Dizzying delight seizes my thoughts, and my body melts in agreement, liquid warmth pooling at my center, dampening my inner thighs. Nature's oldest, most primal plea.

I squeeze him, wanting to answer that call, and he groans, hips bucking up to meet my palm. "Then why won't you kiss me?" I demand, then quickly amend because he has kissed me, just not the way I want, "*Really* kiss me?"

"Because if I start, I won't be able to stop." His mouth is hot near mine, hovering but not descending, one infuriating hair's width from mine.

I nip at his bottom lip, squeezing a little harder, before gliding my hand along his length. "And yet, you put my hand here." I dare him to refute me as I deliver sweet torture. "I think you need it."

His next exhale is ragged, and his hips make another jerking motion. "I do. I need you." It's the longing and the heat in his voice, and none of last night's discomfort or defeat, that makes me believe this is possible. That we can make it work.

Softly, I point out, "You didn't stop once today." And he'd slept the whole night through at the inn. It's the kindest his body has treated him since we've met.

"I didn't. But I didn't come over here to seduce you while you were upset and…"

"Shh." I release my hold on his member to raise a finger to his lips. "Be honest with me. How do you feel?"

His hands tighten in my hair. "Like I might burn to ash if I don't get inside you. But more to your point, I feel…good. More myself, more in control."

"Is this reprieve not a sign? A blessing? Maybe we could take advantage of it. That is, if you'd be willing to try. We can take it slow, and if you need to stop, no matter how abrupt, you won't hurt my feelings. And it won't diminish my desire for you. It never has."

This time when he kisses me, there's nothing chaste about it.

His lips find mine, hot and heavy and searching, all that pent up longing finally unleashed. And yet, even in his harsh command of my mouth, he takes his time, navigating, then mapping its shape. I follow his lead, arcing needily into him, grasping the collar of his shirt. With a gentle nudge from his tongue, he parts my lips, staking his claim. He leaves no part unexplored, each pass of his tongue a wonderfully lewd and sensuous dance.

My chest is heaving when I break for air.

"Wicked temptress," he teases.

"Surely it's you who's ensnared me."

A light tug on my hair, and he angles my head back, inked fingers stroking the column of my throat, exposed, vulnerable, and ghostly pale. "Maybe you're right," he says with something akin to reverence. "Do you like being at my mercy?"

The fire he's sparked is a blazing inferno, and it's a wonder I can still stand.

"I crave it."

He swipes his tongue along my throat before plundering my mouth further, and I sink my fingers into his hair, clenching it as he had mine. Now that I have him, I won't let go.

An intrepid hand finds my breast, pausing to knead it through fabric. When I return the favor by cupping the hardened flesh between his thighs, he wrenches his mouth from mine and takes my hand. "Come with me."

Away from the horses and tent, Elin lays out a blanket for us, making a bed out of the flattened moor grasses beneath. "It's just you and me," he says, pausing to look skyward, serenity falling over his expression. "And the stars to witness what we do here tonight."

I draw him in for another kiss, this time a soft and slow outpouring of affection, and I hope he can feel every ounce, because he deserves to know how I cherish him, even if I'm not brave enough to say it. And it's as I kiss him that my hands busy themselves with the buttons of his waistcoat, working them loose, and push the garment off his shoulders. His neckerchief, then broadcloth shirt, are conquered next, the latter untucked from high-waist trousers and lifted over his head. Disrobing breaks our kiss only a moment before we reach for each other again.

Strip after strip, clothing falls to the ground, our hands working in tandem to free him of his, then mine. He stumbles over none of it, not my home-spun dress, the stays, the chemise, nor the men's trousers I scandalously wear underneath. We don't stop until there's nothing between us, and only then do we part, taking a half step back to feast our eyes on what was hidden.

His sharp intake of breath ignites me with buzzing anticipation.

The moon has painted Elin in soft, cool tones. He's a landscape of lean muscle, a beautiful tapestry of freckled skin, and the night has done nothing to obscure his desire.

"It's like you were carved from stone," I say, tracing my fingers over a hard nipple to the firm stretch of abdominal muscle below, making him shiver. Sea rock made smooth by crashing waves and time. There are scars scattered across his torso and arms, some gunpowder burns, others made from cutlass or splintered projectiles. The war had tried to kill him so many times before we'd met, and he'd survived.

"It wasn't an easy life that did that."

"Those days are done," I remind him gently.

"Done and gone," he agrees, taking me by my hips, hands rough with callouses. But I don't mind the rasp against my skin as he plots a course along my body, learning its terrain, or when he lingers on his favorites. "If this is what comes next," he murmurs, inked knuckles pinching and plucking at my nipples, "I'll be well and truly at peace."

They're strange words, but there'll be time to ask about them later. For now, it's enough knowing that the past forfeits its hold while he's in my arms.

I pull him to the blanket he's spread out for us, but rather than lay on top of me as I expect, he ducks down, draping my legs over his shoulders, nuzzling aside my curls with his nose. The act isn't unfamiliar to me, so the surprise passes quickly, and I sink into his care.

A satisfied grunt escapes him when he swipes his tongue over my slick folds, like the first taste of a beloved delicacy. He sucks the sensitive bundle of nerves at the apex, pausing occasionally to delve his tongue into my wet heat, each motion languid and savoring. Pleasure jolts through my body, and of their own volition, my hips cant upwards, seeking more pressure from his attentive mouth. When my movements become more erratic, he splays his right hand across my belly, the inked word "Hold" visible across his knuckles as he keeps me in place.

I watch the way he applies himself capably to the rhythm of my needy, quaking flesh, bracketed snugly between my thighs. Long, dark lashes dust his freckled cheeks, burnished curls ruffled by the breeze. I reach out to touch them, threading my fingers in his hair, holding him to me.

As tremors steal control of my limbs, my mind drifts into a dizzying, pleasurable fog. Time loses all meaning, and the countryside's nighttime symphony—the crickets and rustling moor grasses—fall away into a distant din. Something lovely coils deep in my core.

Deep gasps and moans are our music now.

Every pass of his tongue brings me higher, flying ever closer to the proverbial sun. I'd thought I was on fire before, but this is instant immolation. If Icarus could see me now, would he warn me away, tell me to find a man who didn't have Death nipping at his heels? Or would he beckon me closer to my doom?

So close. So very, very close.

My hold on Elin's hair grows fierce, the rocking of my hips hard and greedy, but he braces his hands around my thighs, taking it all. The summit I'm trying to reach is *right there.* "Elin," I beg, his name a hoarse and throaty whisper.

He flattens his tongue against my sensitive bud, pressing hard before sucking it.

The tightly wound sensation stretching inside me snaps, and I'm falling down, down, down, screaming through annihilating pleasure. Elin rides out my climax like a seasoned sailor weathers a storm. Or maybe he's the deep-sea creature that plays in its raging waves.

When my mind, body, and soul return to earth, I find he's watching me, brown eyes made dark by the night, both glittering and hungry. He's still working my flesh, lapping up the mess I've made, but there's a smug lift to the corners of his mouth.

He knows he's my undoing.

"Come here," I demand, and he chuckles, finally relinquishing his feast.

Swiping a hand across his chin, he crawls on top of me, settling in the cradle of my hips. Between our bodies, his cock is pinned, throbbing and insistent.

"You came apart so prettily for me," Elin murmurs against my mouth, snaking an arm beneath me.

"Now, it's my turn to watch you unravel." When I reach for his turgid flesh, he lifts himself up just enough to grant me access and holds my gaze as I align him to my entrance, the tip easily slipping inside.

"There's nothing I want more," he says, hitching my leg around his waist, "than to share this with you." Kissing me softly, he rocks into me, coaxing himself deeper, and with each stroke I rise to meet him. There's little resistance, but we savor this moment, taking it slowly and carefully, until he's fully seated inside, our most secret parts flush.

A moan escapes me. We've barely started and yet I'm intoxicated by the feel of him.

His smile is luminous. "Is ceol mo chroí thú."

My stomach flutters at the endearment. *The music of his heart.*

"What beautiful sounds you make," he continues, setting a steady rhythm.

I smooth my hands over the slope of his shoulders, down to his narrow waist, watching his muscles bunch and release.

Countless stars wink overhead, bearing witness to the sweet way Elin claims me. It's a far better sight than the inn's rafters, and there's something so undeniably right about this moment and this setting. That this is the way it was always meant to be.

Sucking a finger into his mouth, then bringing the moistened pad to my sensitive bud, he thrusts harder. We're a chorus of gasps and moans, my nails digging into his backside, urging him on. "That's it," I say. "Just like that."

His eyes are hooded, but he's watching me intently. "Was trying to be a gentleman—chase away the sadness in your eyes, see you safe in bed. But look at this. You got me right where you wanted me." He punctuates the point by grinding his hips into mine, rotating them round and round in maddeningly slow circles. "And what am I to do about that? Can't go back to not having your sweet cunny."

Unexpectedly, my channel gives a loud, happy squelch, but it only drives him into a frenzy, pounding me at a furious pace. "You're the one who called me wife," I challenge, matching his vigor. "Dear, sweet, husband."

We're no such thing, but it does something to him, if the rough curse he shouts is any indication. "Milk me dry," he growls in my ear, and I clench all around him.

Tensing, he stills, brow bunching and lips falling slack. Then he abruptly pulls out, jerking his slick cock as his release spurts across my belly.

When he's finished, he kisses me ferociously, trapping me with his body's delicious weight. "If I were ever to have a wife," he says, slipping one, then two fingers inside me, his thumb working the bundle of nerves. "It'd be you. Now, come for me, *would-be-wife*. One more time."

My body releases upon command.

CHAPTER 9

The next morning, I wake to birdsong and Elin's kisses trailing down my neck. He nips at my collarbone before his face disappears into the valley between my breasts. I ruffle his hair, laughing sleepily, until his lips close around a nipple, dragging out moans instead.

Every tug from his lips and swirling motion from his tongue shoots pleasure straight to my core, and what one hardened peak gets, the other does, too. He's as thorough with my breasts as he was with my cunt the night before, and it's not long until I'm wet and aching.

"Elin," I whimper, clutching his head as he sucks long and hard.

A muffled grunt is the only sign I get that he's heard.

More bruising suction, and my back arcs, pressing a breast more firmly to his mouth. My whimpering has turned to sharp keening. Elin releases my nipple with a loud pop, blowing air lightly across its reddened tip. "Shh, love. I'm going to make it feel better. Be a good girl for me and part your legs."

They're already spread, but I widen them further, eager to fulfill his softly spoken command.

Sliding between my thighs, he fits his cock to my entrance and eases himself in. With how readily my body welcomes him, he's fully seated in one smooth slide. The motion of his hips is a slow churn, colliding with my aching bud by design and stirring up decadent sensations.

Threading his fingers through mine, he places an affectionate kiss to the back of my hand before raising it above my head. He holds us like that, nuzzling his nose to mine, as his hips work their magic. Contentment washes over me, and something light and fluttery warms my chest.

There's no rush to get on the road. No deadline, no milestone to meet. Home will always be there, waiting. We can stay like this until the noonday sun has come and gone. Or longer. We have forever if we choose it.

And yet, our mutual unraveling comes all too soon. What begins as sleepy lovemaking morphs into a frantic race toward release. His hips fly faster, my nails dig into his back, leaving red scratches in their wake. Soft sighs become guttural grunts and moans, more animal than human, marking our descent into primal need. Wet skin slaps, and Elin bites the juncture between shoulder and neck. It should hurt, but it only spurs me on, giving as good as I get.

I tumble headlong into oblivion first, Elin's fingers bringing me over that ledge, and he soon follows, thrusting in hard before tearing himself away, spilling his sticky finish onto my breasts.

"Good God, those were taunting me," Elin grins, pecking one nipple, then the other with a kiss. "Woke up hard enough, but between those pretty little sighs you make while you sleep, and your breasts pressed together…"

"Left you no choice, did it?" I tease.

"Well, if you hadn't roused, I would've marched my naked arse out and taken care of business on my own. But fortune was on my side."

"Glad it was."

Whether it's me, the years trapped at sea, or both, Elin is insatiable.

We clean up, but barely finish the dressing when he ducks his head under my skirts to coax out another orgasm with his wickedly talented mouth. He yanks back open his trousers, stroking himself at a brutal pace until he has to hold me upright because convulsions have stolen the strength from my limbs. But, when we're finished, judging by the release streaking the dirt at my feet, he had no trouble getting off without the use of his hands. I think my pleasure brings him satisfaction.

Sated at last, or at least for now, we set our clothes to right.

"If you start on breakfast, I'll fetch kindling," I offer, smoothing my dress.

"I'll get the horses watered and fed, too."

When I turn to leave, he grabs my wrist, pulling me in for a slow, lazy kiss. "Hurry back," he says after he's released me. The way he stares at my mouth, like something he wants to devour, I'm not certain we'll get any riding done today. At least, not the kind that involves horses.

I hurry off, eager to get back, a giddy smile taking permanent residence on my face.

I'm a distance from camp, a bundle of small branches and twigs in hand, when Death speaks, startling them right out of my arms.

"Bold choice, Éireann. Bedding a doomed man."

"Was it?" I snap, hating how quickly he's soured a good morning. Should've known Death wouldn't let my newfound intimacy with Elin pass without remark. "I saw my future with him."

"But humans are so fragile, and possibility isn't fate."

"You're insufferable. Do you have something useful to say, or are you just here to annoy me?"

"What makes you think what I've said isn't useful?"

I don't sense a vision coming on, so there's that at least.

Rolling my eyes, I ask, "Is it boredom? Is the weight of eternity becoming tedious?" Why else would he waste so much of his time on one man?

Death chuckles. *"On the contrary. While I find this quite amusing, there's plenty keeping me entertained."*

"Then go be entertained elsewhere and leave us alone."

"Can't. We've a wager, remember?"

"We've been over this already. We don't. And. You. Can't. Have. Him."

"Éireann?"

Elin. Had he heard me?

"Who're you talking to?"

I curse under my breath.

"No one." I plaster a smile on my face and calmly turn around. "Do you need something?"

"Just wanted to make sure you were all right."

"I'm quite well. Everything's fine."

Although he doesn't press, I don't think he believes me.

His expression is oddly resigned.

CHAPTER 10

Elin's been gone longer than usual.

The next two days on the road have been rough, and I've gotten used to the regular stops again, but it's been at least an hour. Sunset is quickly approaching, but if we'd stopped to make camp, he would've said so.

I debate what to do, torn between giving him his privacy and making sure he's okay. It's ridiculous, this worry, because I would've foreseen it if he was in trouble, but not every struggle has to be life threatening. And that's what decides it, propelling me into action.

There's a stream nearby, and after tethering our horses, I head in that direction, tracing his path through the brush. I'm noisy in my approach, giving him ample opportunity to call me off. He doesn't.

I find him at the stream vigorously scrubbing a pair of trousers, stripped down to his drawers. They're dyed black, something I've never seen until him, but I see the wisdom in it, knowing what getting out menstrual stains is like, even with access to chloride of lime. Next to him, draped across a log, are an identical set of black drawers, freshly laundered and set aside to dry.

I crouch upstream of him, and gesture to the dirt-streaked shirt balled up by his feet. "May I?"

His cheeks stain pink, but he nods, and I set to washing it, helping myself to the soap he's got. Suds build then get carried away by the current. Wash, dunk, wash, dunk.

One more good rinse should do it.

I plunge my hands into the cold water, pushing the billowing cloth down, but instead of a cloud of white bubbles, the stream blooms red with blood. Gasping, I snatch my hands back.

Elin abandons his task to take my hands, searching for something that isn't there. "You cut?"

He saw it, saw the blood. Folks sometimes could. "I…"

I want to enjoy this moment, caught by the earnest concern in his eyes, the closeness of his bare body, our hands locked together. It's a spark that could ignite into something more. Something tender and feeling a lot like love.

But something's coming. Something bad. And there's no time to waste.

I tear myself away from him, though it pains me to do so in his moment of vulnerability, and I run.

There's another vision coming. It's itching at the back of my skull, blurring my eyes, but I keep running through the heather, daring not to stop. The last warning didn't give me much of a head start.

We're back on the road. But we're not alone. There are riders, five of them, and they're a nasty bunch demanding Elin's coin purse at gunpoint. One of them I recognize—the drunken ruffian from the inn with the red neckerchief. Greedy bastard doesn't care that it's all we have left to buy our passage home.

We're outnumbered, but Elin is calm, almost serene on top of his horse. It's strangely beautiful, this self-assuredness in the face of danger.

In a quick draw, he whips up his pistol and fires. He hits one, draws a second pistol and shoots again. Two of the highwaymen fall to the ground, but the others fire their own shots. One misses, whizzing by. Another grazes Elin's arm and the third hits his leg. He grunts, but tosses his guns aside, unsheathing a Navy-issue cutlass. He charges and cuts down two more while they fumble to reload—he's so quick and efficient, there's no second of hesita-

tion, but even as swiftly as he's moving, the last highwayman, the one with the red neckerchief, raises his gun.

The next bullet buries in Elin's stomach.

The vision fades, and I sprint the rest of the way to my horse, wrestling the reins free from the tree I tied it to. I swing into the saddle, and with a kick, speed off, not once looking behind me.

It's dark when I find the band of ruffians, the moon dipping in and out between clouds. The way one of them has paused to crouch over a set of hoofprints makes me think they've been tracking us from the inn. Apparently, paying off the red neckerchief-wearing one was an enticement, rather than a deterrent, in the long run.

A foolish mistake, and one I won't be making again.

It's easy to lead them away from where I'd left Elin. Just a little flash of skin is all it takes. These men are basic creatures after all, begging for the slightest perceived sign of seduction, making invitations out of thin air. When we're far enough away that I'm sure Elin won't hear, I dismount.

I can smell the sea now, carried in on the wind, though I can't see it.

We're nearing the crossing that'll bring us to our journey's end, and I won't fail now, not for anything. This is my mistake to fix.

Wrapping my arms around myself, I drift forward a little, putting distance between myself and my horse, trying not to think too much about what comes next. But I'm getting Elin home, no matter what it takes. Nothing's worth his life, not even an act branding me as a woman of loose morals.

The highwaymen jump down from their horses. They chuckle and jostle amongst themselves, vying for the first go. I think they draw straws.

Boots crunch along the ground, their collective presence looming hot at my back and souring my stomach.

One of them whistles, long and shrill.

"Come here, lass! A kiss for 'ol Tom."

I hate that they're mocking the North Dubliner accent. It's damn right offensive.

Trembling, I take another step, just one more. That's all I need.

"Oi! Where ya think you're…"

"What the…"

Sliding, tumbling rock is followed by shouting. And the shouting quickly turns into a symphony of screaming, long and dimming.

Then sudden silence.

My breath expels ragged, but relieved. I turn, empty air kissing the soles of my feet as I drift back to solid ground. I don't bother looking down. All that matters is the highwaymen didn't see the cliff I lured them to, and Elin is safe.

There's a dark chuckle. *"How far will you go to defy fate?"*

As far as it takes.

"Heard screaming. You all right?" Elin asks it nonchalantly, but it's clear he threw on wet clothes to race after me. There's an opening in the clouds for now, the moon peeking through, so I can see how they cling to him, even in the dark.

"Better. How'd you find me?"

"Hoof prints." He looks over my shoulder, then back at me. "I was good at tracking. Before."

I don't dare say anything to that—I've just killed five men—but he doesn't press. Whatever pieces he puts together, don't send him running.

We make camp, but when it's time to sleep, he hesitates outside the tent.

I'm not sure why he does. Maybe it's the state I found him in at the stream. It's cooled his ardor and has struck a lethal blow to his pride. Or maybe he knows I'm an unapologetic murderess and that's given him pause.

However, I choose to believe it's the former.

"You can't go to bed in wet clothes," I say, ducking inside to get myself situated. "Won't be anything I haven't seen, anyways."

"Right." He disappears for a moment, but when he returns, he's just in his drawers.

Crawling into his bedroll, he shifts onto his back and stares up, thoughtful.

I want to ask him what's on his mind, but I'm afraid to. Both because of what I've done and what his condition's return might mean for us. I don't need him to regularly bed me, if that's what he's worried about, but what if he retreats, anyways? Thinks himself unworthy of any affection?

I'm debating what to say to reassure him.

After a time, he turns to look at me, expression soft. "Thank you for today," he says, holding out his hand.

It surprises me, but I take it, never wanting to let go.

And the knowing look he gives me steals my breath away. He knows what I did, I'm sure of it, and yet, he's grateful. I swallow thickly, not letting the tears that mist my eyes fall, because I'm grateful, too. Grateful for him, and that tonight has ended as it has, with him alive and well.

That's how we fall asleep, with his hand in mine.

At some point in the night our bodies gravitate toward one another, seeking warmth and comfort. The new day finds me nestled in Elin's arms and neither of us hurry to part. When I burrow closer, he presses a kiss to my temple, and whispers that he loves me, almost too quiet to hear.

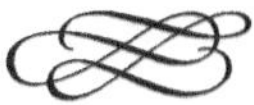

CHAPTER 11

It's while cooking breakfast that I see it.

Elin's crouched before the fire, smiling to himself as he stokes the flames. Behind him, where the tent should be, I see a church yard, dotted by headstones and yew trees standing sentry. The worst omen yet.

And the foretelling hits me fast.

He's burning with fever, too weak to leave his bed. He can't keep anything down and from his bowels comes dark blood. This is not an old man I see, but a man cut down in his prime, wasting away on a narrow bed, and from a dire illness he's had all along.

I flee from camp, before he can see. Before he can hear.

Please let him not hear.

A wail rises in my throat, such body wrenching agony as I collapse to my knees, nails digging into my thighs. What emerges is an ugly sound as my heart rends in two. The grief is real even if the wail is unbidden.

Elin's not just sick.

His body is slowly dying.

We were on this path all along. The runaway horse, the bog, the band of ruffians—all real threats, but they hid the inevitable—distractions giving me false hope.

I was never going to save him.

"Why?" I yell to Death, pulling my hair by the roots. *"Why show me love when you knew this would happen? And then insult me with a wager?"*

"Because you can still save him." There's none of his usual taunting. Death's tone is gentle. Reassuring, even. And it makes no sense. Would he truly be cruel enough to continue toying with me while I'm in anguish?

"Éireann!"

Swiping tears from my eyes, I see Elin sprinting toward me, sharp and alert, his pistol in hand. He must've thought I was in danger.

"Éireann!" He falls to his knees at my side. "What happened?" Checking me over for injury, and finding none, he envelops me in his arms, face pressed into my neck, nose buried in my hair. He holds me so tight it's almost painful.

"How?" I beg. *"How do I save him?"*

Death replies, *"If you kiss him beneath the shade of a yew tree, he will live, but your spirits will be entwined forever."*

"What does that mean?"

"He will never die."

Elin says my name again, soft but grave. "It's time, isn't it?"

"Time?" My voice is shaky.

"My time to die."

Surprise chokes me. "You know?"

"From the moment I saw you." He tenderly tucks my hair behind my ear. "My mother would tell me these stories, stories I'd forgotten about until I saw your face. And I just knew. The stories were real."

Tears spring to my eyes anew, a sob building in my throat. "Why didn't you say anything?" I choke out.

"Because you were as reluctant as I, Bean-Sídhe." It's our peoples' word for what I am. A banshee. He holds me while my shoulders heave with grief. "I'm sorry I never made it back home, but I'm not afraid. Not with you by my side."

No. We've made it this far, I'm not giving up now. Not when there's still a fight we can win.

Sniffling, I pull back just enough to meet his eyes. "There's a way. We can save you." I cup his cheeks, hope and determination chasing away my tears. "Follow me to the yew tree."

He meets my gaze unblinking. I can see the confusion. The wariness. He doesn't know what that means, and why should he? I must sound like I'm raving. "Will it heal me?"

"He'll be as he is," Death answers before I can fumble. *"Frozen in time. But it won't get worse."*

I brush hair from his eyes—absently thinking that it'll need trimming soon, and that we'll have plenty of time to get it cut. "No," I reply truthfully. "But you'd be immortal."

And it's not until I see the reservation in his eyes that I realize that might not be the boon I think it is. That Elin might choose death over living an eternity with his condition.

No, no, no, please, don't leave me. I'm begging him silently, but it's not my decision. It's not me who has to live with it.

"I need some time to think about this."

"Okay." My voice is barely above a whisper. I can't tell if it's a platitude, or if he really means to consider it. I'm perilously teetering somewhere between hope and despair.

"I don't presume to know what you're thinking. It might be that this should be an easy decision, and I wish it was. Sometimes I loathe this body, and the way it humiliates me, the things it makes me feel. Defiled, debased, so very sick..." He rubs a thumb across his inked knuckles. "I've held on this long, but I don't know if I can do it forever."

My heart shatters into pieces at his words. Even though I want to run and hide and mourn, I hug him fiercely, like it might be the last time.

If he chooses the way I fear, I'll not spend the rest of my eternal life with regret. I'll hold him now and as often as he'll allow.

I'll hold him until the end.

CHAPTER 12

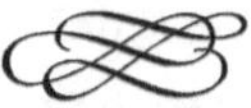

Elin asks for solitude and ventures off to contemplate my offer.

There's nothing to do but give it to him.

I'm a miserable wreck waiting, my stomach in knots, but it's his choice and his alone. I'll not try to sway him or make him believe love will be enough.

This isn't about me, or what I can give him.

I take long walks alone, wandering aimlessly. I yank out moor grasses by the fistful and let them go to see how far the wind can carry them away. Hours and hours go by occupied with all sorts of nonsensical things. But more often, absolutely nothing at all, except staring blankly at the sky and begging fate to be kinder to us both. Maybe making peace with losing him would be a better use of my time, but I can't bring myself to take that plummet just yet.

My nights are sleepless. I jolt awake at every noise, not wanting to miss the sound of Elin's returning footsteps.

"I've never seen you like this."

Dare I say, Death sounds worried.

I laugh bitterly. "Haven't you?"

Once upon a time, I was just as human and mortal as Elin,

scratching out a meager living in a cruel, unforgiving world. Seems so long ago and distant. A life that belonged to another, these memories fickle and few.

But the tragedy remains. As it always does.

When a harsh winter claimed my entire village—my mama, my papa, my siblings, and my nieces and nephews—Death had given me a choice. Join them or become his faithful servant. A Bean-Sídhe. Death's own herald.

I did not want to die before I had a chance to live, and so I chose to serve.

For centuries, I've seen death before it comes, warned people before they died, witnessed their final moments. And it hurt every time. The wail is as much as a calling card as it is genuine grief. For me, to live and to serve Death is to mourn.

"Not this bad. You've never loved anyone like him."

I loved my family, I can remember that at least, but that's not what Death means. He's never seen me in love before.

"There was never the chance," I say, but that's not quite right. "I never considered it might be possible."

My presence, my purpose, at its essence is a harbinger of doom. Nothing more, nothing less.

Some people know what I am in their final moments. Some don't. But Elin did. From the very first moment he saw me he knew what I was, and what that meant for him. And yet he traveled with me. Offered me shelter, a place by his side. He let me in, sharing the painful parts of his past and his calamitous present.

He called me his wife and made love to me beneath the stars.

"Why didn't you tell me about the yew tree from the start?"

Death pauses. I know he's still there because I can feel his shadowy presence. *"You needed to learn to fight for him,"* he says, after a time. *"Falling in love is easy. But loving, truly loving someone, is hard."*

Those are knowing words.

"You speak from experience." The revelation shocks me.

"It's beautiful though, despite the struggle."

And then he's gone.

Days pass.

Maybe it's delirium from a lack of sleep, but the acute ache of Elin's absence has numbed, granting me a weird imitation of peace. I'm leaning against the wide trunk of a tree, staring at a sunrise, the prettiest I've seen in a while, when I feel a tap on my shoulder.

I turn, heart in my throat.

Elin is standing behind me, holding out a bouquet of wildflowers.

"Elin?" I cradle them in my arms, touched because they're a precious gift. Terrified because this might be goodbye.

"Forever is a long time," he begins, and the soothing, gentling way he speaks drives spikes of fear into my heart. As if he means to soften the blow of bad news.

I can't speak. Can't think. If this is the end, I'm not ready. I didn't prepare for his refusal, because I couldn't bear to put the cart before the horse on my grief.

"I don't know what forever looks like for you, for me, for us," he continues. "But I don't know what death looks like either and that's just as final." He takes a step closer to me, cupping my cheeks wet with tears. "All I know is what's happening right now. That I'm falling in love with you, and I finally have a chance to live a life of my choosing. I know what we have is new, but I'm at peace every time we're together. And maybe it makes me a hopeless, gambling fool, but I want to take a chance on that."

My breath catches in my throat, mind whirring, not daring to misinterpret. "Are you saying…"

"I'll follow you." His voice is so soft and yet so certain as he slides a hand into my raven-dark hair, cradling the back of my head. "I'll follow you to the yew tree."

His lips fall to mine, all warmth and hopeful promise.

Relief crashes into me and then, in the moment before I close my eyes to sink into his embrace, I see it.

It doesn't look like the ones we have back home. That's why I didn't notice before, but I know it in my heart now.

The ancient tree Elin kisses me beneath is the one that binds us.

EPILOGUE

SPRING 2016, THE ENGLISH COUNTRYSIDE

Centuries pass. And time has been kind to Elin.

Specialized medicine has improved by leaps and bounds, and because of it, he's in remission, and has been for years. What he'd called a bowel calamity in the spring of 1816 is a disease called Pancolitis in 2016. It's an autoimmune condition, which means Elin's immune system attacks healthy tissue, and having it increases the risk of developing colon cancer.

It nearly claimed his life all those years ago.

But we fought fate and won.

There's a tap on my shoulder.

"New dress?"

I turn and find Elin standing right behind me, smiling, his fiery curls backlit by the morning sun.

He looks the same as the day I met him, but happier, healthier, and decorated with a lot more tattoos—some he's done himself.

But our favorite is the ancient English yew tree that spans his back. The very same as the one we stand beneath now, blanketing us in its shade. The one that not only bound us but gave us centuries of love and a life Elin chose.

"Bought it at the airport." I swish the skirts coquettishly about my bare legs. "Like it?" It's tight in some places, flowy in others, but the features that are most strikingly different to my dresses of two hundred years ago are its thin straps and a hemline that falls above the knee.

"I love it." The heat in his gaze tells me he'd love to take it off more.

And yet, he takes my hands and bows his head to mine, staring intently into my eyes. "Hold Fast" is still inked across his knuckles, the lines as sharp as ever. It doesn't fade, doesn't blur. Just boldly defies the passage of time. Just like Elin.

"Happy Anniversary, mo chroí," I say.

His lips curl into a sweet smile as he gazes at my mouth. "Tourists aren't due for another thirty minutes," he murmurs. "How would you like it if I flipped up that pretty little dress and had you right here?"

My cheeks heat. We've gotten bolder in the things we try over the years but risking getting caught never fails to make me blush. And ridiculously aroused. Something he knows abundantly well, the mischievous devil.

Raising onto my toes, I lean in to kiss him.

He captures my face in both hands, stroking the column of my throat with his thumbs as he slowly sips at my mouth, savoring each taste. Despite the filthiness of his intentions, it's a tender dance of lips pursued by the languid glide of tongue, and the easy tempo endures even when he presses me against the tree, trapping my body with his. The way he sucks my lower lip into his mouth, tugging lightly with his teeth, is so deliciously obscene, I whimper when he abruptly pulls away, leaving me aching.

His eyes hold mine as he sucks two of his fingers into his mouth, cheeks hollowing out, before pulling the wet digits free and reaching under my dress. In one swift motion, he deftly shoves my panties aside, sliding his fingers through wet folds. "Been thinking about me?"

My breath hitches. "Always."

He rolls his fingers over my clit, then delves them one by one inside me, never looking away. "Your eyes dilate when I do that," he comments, looking from one to the other. Above my head, he braces his other arm against the tree, those fingers curling lightly and affectionately through my hair.

"Yours do, too." They're so dark a brown it's sometimes hard to tell, but the early morning sun illuminates just enough of the boundary between iris and pupil for me to see that his are blown wide.

"It's because I missed you," he says against my lips, catching a moan as he churns in and out of me in short, measured strokes, the heel of his hand delivering delicious pressure against my clit. "And because I like making you feel good."

These days my duties as a Bean-Sídhe are focused on helping people avoid their preventable, untimely deaths. It's rewarding work, but it sometimes takes me away from Elin for weeks at a time.

It's been three since we've last seen each other, making us especially eager.

Pressed against the tree's smooth bark, I tilt my head back and let the sensations Elin draws out take reign, trusting him to swiftly bring me over the edge. What Elin does is an artform, and more than two lifetimes have made him a master at delivering carnal promises.

Birds twitter cheerfully overhead, but I dimly register it. Elin's breath at my ear, coupled with my own gasping, is the symphony I fall apart to.

"Such a lovely mess you've made for me." He shows how I've coated his fingers, then sucks them clean.

Bliss makes my movements heavy. My head lolls, coming to rest against his arm. "Make another for me?"

He kisses my mouth hard, before wrenching away, tugging his shirt over his head. He spreads it on the ground and beckons me to lay down.

I'm all too eager to comply.

Once I'm situated and comfortable, he kneels between my legs, unzipping his fly. Heat flares low in my belly watching his inked fingers work over the hard bulge. With a sharp tug down, he frees himself—ruddy cock jutting proudly between us.

"Unbutton the top for me," he says, palming his shaft and giving it a lazy stroke. "I want to see those pretty tits bounce."

I spring into action, prying open the first four buttons. I've always loved the command in his voice. Time hasn't changed that.

"Good girl," he praises, hiking the skirt up to my navel. Then whisking aside my panties, he presses a quick kiss to my sodden flesh, and lines himself up. He gives me his weight, forearms bracketing my head as he eases in, as unhurried as he'd been our first time. A memory I replay over and over in my mind, so I never forget.

"I never tire of this," he says into the slope of my neck, steadily moving his hips.

"Me neither." My toes curl into the dewy moor grass. "Swear I love it more every time."

He cups a breast, pinching and pulling at the nipple. The other bounces between us in time to the rocking motion of our bodies.

The sun's growing warmth on our skin has me sneaking a glance at my watch. "It's 7:45," I announce. The first tour bus comes at 8:00.

"Guess we better be quick then," he says, taking that very same wrist and pinning it above my head, near a flowering cluster of Lily of the Valley. His hips move faster, working us up to a punishing pace that's more fitting for the situation.

"Just when I thought you didn't know the meaning of a quickie," I tease, but gasp when he hits a particularly good spot.

Noting the reaction, he continues thrusting at the angle that produced it. "And why would I rush when you feel this good?"

I huff a laugh. Can't argue with that.

And yet, Elin proceeds with greater urgency, throwing his whole body into each driving thrust. The moans it knocks out of me are deep, guttural things, and it's not long before he sends me hurtling into sweet oblivion again.

"That's it, squeeze me." As if on command, my channel clamps all around him. "Good girl." His hips buck forward, and then he stiffens.

Sated, he collapses on top of me and nuzzles my cheek. "Happy 200th."

"Happy 200th."

When he pulls out, a rush of warmth follows, but he yanks a handkerchief from his back pocket and wipes me clean.

The distant sound of wheels, and an accompanying dirt cloud billowing up from the road beyond has us springing to our feet. We can't see the vehicle yet—it being somewhere over the crest of a hill—but it won't be long now. We hurry to right our clothing.

Moments later, the tour bus rolls up, whistles and cheers ringing from its open windows. Elin's zipped up, but his shirt's a crumpled mess in his hand, and my dress is askew, the buttons all mismatched in my frantic haste to get them fastened. No doubt my hair's thoroughly mussed, too.

Blushing furiously, I offer a shy, little wave, but Elin just pulls a leaf from my hair with an affectionate wink, unbothered by the audience, and takes my hand. "Got us a room at the inn," he says, kissing my cheek. "And I think you have some making up to do for rushing this, mo chroí."

I swat playfully at his chest but don't deny that it's exactly what I want to do, too.

After all, it's been three weeks since we've last seen each other.

What they say about distance making the heart grow fonder is true, but we never allow it for too long. Forever is just the right amount of time, and we mean to make the most of it.

Elin leads me to a motor scooter parked nearby. After we don our helmets, I climb behind him, wrapping my arms around his waist. As the engine rumbles to life, I twist in my seat, blowing a kiss to the tree we owe everything to, and with a lurch we speed down the dirt access road, racing off toward our next adventure.

Nestling against his back, I grin to myself.

Wherever he goes, I will follow.

Home is where Elin is.

—THE END—

Thank you for reading! Did you enjoy? Please add your review because nothing helps an author more and encourages readers to take a chance on a book than a review.
For first looks at covers, character art, and more, sign up for my newsletter at www.dmniccoli.com.

ACKNOWLEDGMENTS

A lot of wonderful people helped bring this book to life, and I'm so grateful for the thoughtfulness and care with which they handled Elin's and Éireann's story. I really put my heart on my sleeve with this one.

The biggest, most heartfelt thanks to my beta readers Alexandra, Katie Erin, Morgan, Sarah, and Seffra. I'm continually blown away by your insightful feedback and support. You knew just when and where to push, and where to encourage. This book shines because of you.

Thank you, Kyle, for all the late-night brainstorming sessions and for helping me map out the events of this book when I decided it needed to be a novella instead of a short story. And thank you Agatha Andrews for encouraging me to write this as it needed to be written.

Jessica S. Taylor your breadth of indie publishing knowledge is astounding. Thank you so much for sharing it with me. It's made getting this book out into the big, wide world a whole lot easier.

Julia Laurel, you're an absolute artistic genius. Thank you for illustrating such a beautiful cover. It's dreamy and whimsical and so full of meaningful little details that makes this author's heart sing. Please know that the tender, loving care and time you put into this piece is very well cherished.

To my agent Kaitlyn Katsoupis, thank you for always having my back and for supporting my work no matter where it ends up. Your encouragement of hybrid authoring means a lot to me, and so does your generosity and advice. Thank you for your editorial feedback on this story, for testing novella submissions in traditional publishing waters, and for showing the utmost love for my monsters and vicious ladies.

And last, but far from least, my mom. This book is for us. Thank you for braving an early read and for going on this journey with Elin, Éireann, and I. I hope I've done you, our family, and this story proud. I love you so much.

xoxo
Desirée

ABOUT THE AUTHOR

By night, Desirée M. Niccoli writes a blend of vicious romance and cozy horror, featuring monsters, villains, and the supernatural, often served with (mostly) emotionally intelligent characters and heart. By day, she is a public relations professional living the nomadic military life with her husband and two cats Pawdry Hepburn and Puma Thurman. Although born and raised in Pittsburgh, Desirée has since lived in coastal Maine (where her spooky heart truly lies), Maryland, and Connecticut.

Want to be the first to get a look at covers, sneak peeks, and more? Sign up for her newsletter and find out more at www.dmniccoli.com.

facebook.com/dmniccoli.com

x.com/dmniccoli

instagram.com/author_dmniccoli

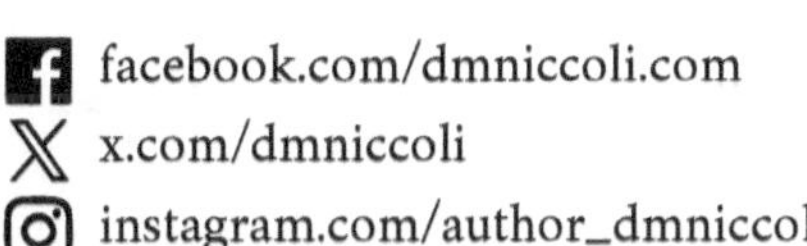

PUBLISHED WORKS

<u>Haven Cove Series</u>
Called to the Deep
Song of Lorelei

<u>Standalones</u>
Given to the Ghoul

<u>Short Stories</u>
"Meat Cute,"
Brigids Gate Press,
Dangerous Waters: Deadly Women of the Sea anthology
"The Feast of Dead Man's Hollow,"
Brigids Gate Press
Crimson Bones anthology